# WALT DISNEY'S

# ALICE
## *in*
## WONDERLAND

One beautiful spring day, a young girl named Alice sat by the river as her sister read aloud from a history book. But Alice wasn't really listening. She was playing with her cat, Dinah, and daydreaming.

The sun was bright, and the air was warm. Alice closed her eyes and no longer heard her sister's voice.

When Alice opened her eyes, she was surprised to see a large, white rabbit dash by. She jumped up. The rabbit was wearing a waistcoat and a bow tie and was carrying a huge pocket watch.

"I'm late! I'm late for a very important date," the White Rabbit muttered as he sped along.

Alice went chasing after him, but stopped short at a rabbit hole.

The rabbit scuttled down the hole. Thinking he might be late for something fun, like a party, Alice followed him.

Suddenly, she stumbled and fell head over heels into the hole. But instead of falling quickly, she began to fall slower and slower—until she was floating!

Alice landed just in time to see the rabbit disappear through a tiny door. Alice was too big to follow him. The Doorknob suggested she try the bottle labeled DRINK ME on the table behind her. With each sip, Alice got smaller and smaller.

When she was ready to open the door, the Doorknob told her that it was locked. Then he mentioned she might try a cookie from the box labeled EAT ME. Alice took a bite and began to grow and grow. Soon she was crying giant tears! The Doorknob told her to drink again. She grew smaller and smaller until she floated right through the keyhole!

On the other side of the keyhole, Alice found herself in a wondrous world filled with talking birds and walking fish. She hoped that one of these creatures could help her find the White Rabbit, but they were no help at all.

Soon she came upon some twins named Tweedledum and Tweedledee.

"How do you do, Tweedledum and Tweedledee?" Alice greeted them. She could not tell them apart at all.

"When first meeting someone, you should shake hands and state your name and business," said the twins together, each grabbing one of Alice's hands and shaking it firmly. "That's manners!"

Then, Tweedledee and Tweedledum danced Alice around and around. But they were so rough that they knocked her down. Alice was not pleased.

"Talk about manners!" Alice exclaimed as she picked herself up. "If you must know, my name is Alice, and I'm following the White Rabbit. I'm very sorry, but I must go."

Despite the twins' protests, Alice
went on her way. Soon she found herself
in an unusual garden filled with singing
flowers. The roses, violets, and lilies wel-
comed Alice warmly until a haughty
orchid called her a weed.

"I'm not a weed!" Alice cried, but the
flowers rudely pushed her away. They did
not want her to stay and take root.

Angrily, Alice walked away through
the tall grass. A while later, she spotted
a smiling animal sitting in a tree. At
first, Alice could only see his toothy
grin. Then some stripes appeared, and
finally a face.

At last she saw that he was a cat!
"Oh, I want to go home, but I can't find
my way!" Alice cried.

"That's because you have no way,"
said the Cheshire Cat. "All ways here
are the *Queen's* way!"

And with that, a tunnel magically
appeared in the tree trunk. Alice hur-
ried through it.

On the other side of the tunnel, she saw the White Rabbit. He was about to introduce the Queen of Hearts.

It was not long before the temperamental Queen became annoyed with Alice. "Off with her head!" cried the Queen.

Alice ran for her life. There was a mad chase through Wonderland. Then, out of nowhere, a little door appeared before her. Alice ran to it, but it was locked. She peeked through the keyhole. There, on the other side, she saw herself, asleep under a tree.

"Please wake up, Alice!" she cried.

Suddenly, Alice awoke on the river-
bank.

Alice looked around but didn't see
any strange, talking creatures. All she
saw was her sister, the old history book,
and her cat Dinah. And that was just
fine with Alice.